RONIN

Parts 1-3
The Conquerors of K'Tara
Short Stories

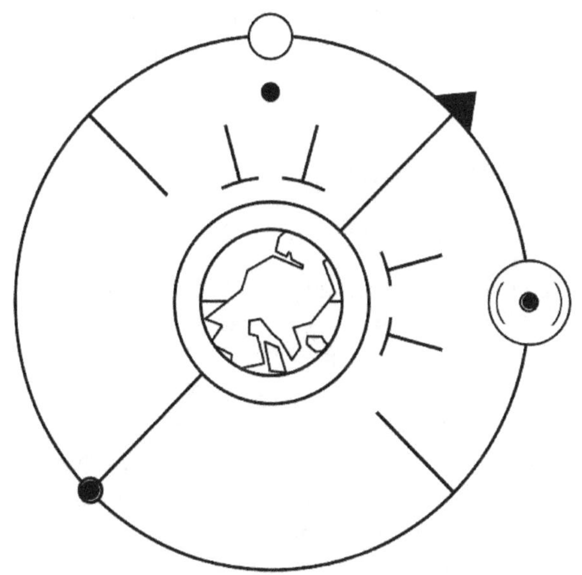

L.A. DI PAOLO

RONIN Parts 1-3 – The Conquerors of K'Tara Short Stories

ISBN: 979-8-9920388-1-1

v9

Ronin had decided to go down into the plains today, and to go there on his own, ignoring everyone's advice, including that of his digimate, and that of his friend Canyon, though the former and the latter had different reasons for trying to dissuade him from his plan. He would go to the old–or, as many might say, decrepit–city of Boulder, where he had heard he could find two things he had been wanting for a long time: try some *realmeat,* and perhaps befriend a fullhuman female–though he had no idea how he might do that. And coming down had been exactly as they had told him it would be: stressful. First the security checks, then the health checks–which were meant not to protect the Downsiders, but to have a baseline to compare him against when he came back, to protect the people from Upside–and finally the briefings where he was forced to waste fifteen minutes listening to a paranoid government official telling him and the other travelers what to do and not to do once Downside, including serious warnings against prolonged physical proximity with the locals and emphatic prohibitions against physical contact with them, especially for Upsiders like him—they were two amongst the dozen attending the briefing— with mostly organic bodies.

The actual trip from Upside to the plains had only taken ten minutes, but he would not have minded it if had taken longer because the view had been absolutely transfixing. Seeing with his own eyes the dropping ridges, the vast expanse of arid land with its amazing reds and tans, and that ancient city at the bottom, seeing all that with his own eyes was so much more exhilarating than anything he had seen in the virtuals.

At destination though–as he came out of the transporter–his guts had tied themselves into worse knots than he had expected. The unfamiliar sounds and foreign faces, the strange heat and sights—all these things felt a little overwhelming to Ronin. Only the presence of a few Control cops–as strange as that might be–in their synthetic coverings, and recognizable forms and faces gave him some measure of comfort. But he had *wanted* to come, had decided to come despite the warnings, and so–after a brief hesitation–he called-up his mind map, searched for the directions to the main market his friend Canyon had told him about, and started walking. As he got going, he initiated a hack Canyon had sent him and used it to return fake signals about his condition and whereabouts to the Planetary Monitoring Agency. The procedure stressed him, but he had tested it with his friend before coming, and it had worked. So, he prayed it would continue to do so here. He also turned off all private communications so that he would not be disturbed by any friend wishing to chat or pry on him during his visit

Downside—a place that had stopped evolving centuries ago already, though it had been the birthplace of humanity.

As he walked, following the directions that manifested in his mind as easily as knowledge he had acquired through personal experience, Ronin started to grab his thumb anxiously. He could call upon facts—bits of information or complex information—at will. And he could manipulate them, process them all with a sense of familiarity, even those that had been implanted in him. But feelings, emotions, subjective things, they still needed to be experienced. So, even though he recognized the facial and body types and the vestments, the impressions that they all left on him—now that he was surrounded by them—were utterly unnerving and overwhelming. But, little by little, the tension lessened until he could walk and cross eyes with those he saw along the way, even if only briefly and with a forced smile.

Thirty minutes later, he stood in front of a ricemeat vendor's booth. The male's skin, like that of every other fullhuman he had seen, was the color of dirt, where it wasn't scarred and blemished by disease and pollution.

After finishing with another customer, the male approached and spoke. Ronin wondered what he was saying. There *were* still people who used their voices to communicate Upside, on the Disk, but the sounds coming out of this male's mouth were incomprehensible.

Ronin made a sign to slow the male down and forced a whisper out of his voicebox, hoping he would be understood. He said, "A juicy one?"

The male shook his head and uttered more unintelligible words directed to his female partner who looked Ronin up-and-down, warmly. Though it initially confused him, her smile infected him too, and he smiled back, even if he did so while eyeing the male diffidently. Then she went indoors, giving him a conspiratorial nod. Did *she* understand him? And was she going to bring him what he had come for? He hoped so and felt some excitement at the thought.

Ronin waited patiently, although the male's scornful smile wiped his earlier excitement off his face. When the male rolled his eyes for the third time, Ronin almost got angry. But it was his own fault, after all. What Upsiders ever came down here to ask for realmeat? Certainly not the proper, law-abiding ones. Only wild ones like his friend Canyon who came to have a blast exploring and enjoying things which weren't available Upside ever did so. Canyon had told him you had to know where to go and how to ask for the animal meat because the food *was* illegal, and even if one wouldn't be *jailed* for being found in possession of it, one could still be fined and shamed for it. This ricemeat vendor was one of them that would sell visitors forbidden products if they knew the code. Had Ronin asked for it incorrectly? He hoped not.

Ronin had come down to the plains for two things: to try real meatflesh, for which he had always had an unexplainable fantasy, and to meet a fullhuman female because he was tired of virtual relationships and visiloves, and he yearned for the type of companionship and love he saw in very old movies, though everyone he knew Upside thought him queer for it.

And although Canyon thought him just as queer, he had accepted Ronin's strangeness and had shown him digirecordings of fullhuman females he had met while on his multiple trips Downside, and had even told Ronin that he would introduce him to a few if he came along with them on their next visit. But Ronin was not the social type, and so, after much time spent motivating and encouraging himself, he had finally decided to do this on his own that very morning.

After about ten minutes, the female vendor came back. She had an eager smile on her pocked, chubby face, and she looked at him with curious eyes. Ronin assumed it was because she had never before seen a smooth-skinned, blond, six-foot tall human, and he blushed. *Why did I do that?!*

There were also three other females standing behind her, one of whom had such bewitching eyes that she looked surprisingly beautiful, and all three were watching him with hands on their mouths, covering giggles. Ronin's eyebrows knitted in a frown; he couldn't tell if they were laughing at him or trying to hide their blushes at seeing a male from Upside. If because of the former, it was his own fault for looking so out-of-place; he should have come with more appropriate clothing. Indeed, he had come down dressed in the tight-fitting, iridescent clothing which were in fashion Upside, whereas the people here were dressed in rather baggy, solid-colored clothes. But the possibility that their reactions were due to the latter cause gave him shivers. Indeed, two of them had excessively predatory eyes in addition to skin blemished and scarred from the conditions on the planet and the continued degeneration of the fullhuman genome due to some viral disease that had infected them a few centuries back. This was one of the reasons physical contact between Upsiders and Downsiders was prohibited, even though he'd seen an official recording, at university, stating that the virus was no longer a threat.

Ronin's eyes lit up when the sandy-haired one, perhaps eighteen, twenty-two, or twenty-six—he could not tell the ages of people down here—moved her hand and showed him a smile which, added to her mesmerizing eyes, troubled him deeply. The fact was, he had only seen such expressions—smiles which covered the entire face—in the movies, and never on the faces of any Upsider, whether neutral, male, or female. The effect was such that her own scars and blemishes were almost—they *were*—beautiful.

Just now, the female vendor said to the male something that sounded like, "Hereyago, luv. Tsforthesider."

He wasn't certain what those words meant, but he could tell from her glances she had come back with what he was looking for. Since his arrival, he had felt out-of-place and uncomfortable interacting with the locals, such as with the child who came to touch him on his way here, and the fullhuman female who then came to retrieve the child with diffident looks and apologetic words; Ronin had not said a word in return or made any motions until the female had left with the child. But now, seeing that little illicit package in the female's hand, he felt a secret excitement, and he ached to be given it, so much so that he looked at the vendors more eagerly than was natural for him to do, and he forced a croaky "please" out of his mouth.

The male replied to the female, who must be his *wife*— people still coupled themselves down here—and said something that sounded like "Thanks, cotcake!" He then took the package carefully, turned toward Ronin and handed it to him, saying, "Your *juicy one*."

Ronin took the package with an almost reverent motion. When his friends found out about this, they would be whizzed. Just now, an unbelievable smell reached his nostrils through the wrapping, and–unable to resist it–he moved to open the package, just enough, to peek inside.

As he did, the ricemeat vendor turned from a darkish tan to a furious red, and he slammed his hand on Ronin's, who froze.

When he realized what he had been about to do, he looked around, expecting a squad of cops to assault him. But there were none, and his heart slowed. He then made careful motions to re-wrap his sandwich properly and completely, and then moved it away from his face to lessen the inviting smell.

Ronin looked back at the vendor with an apologetic smile.

The male said, suddenly, "You should get a bottl' water, too."

"Water? No. Thank you. I'm not thirsty."

The male frowned again then said, "That's fourinhundred."

With another confused expression, Ronin asked the man to repeat himself.

The male did so—annoyance plain on his face—enunciating each word, "Four. Hundred."

Four hundred?! I knew this would be expensive, but four hundred credits? Ronin put his finger on the scanner, paid for his "ricemeat" and made to leave, but something held him back–the girl. He wanted to know her. But, how would he know her? He wished he could invite her to follow him. But what would they do? He couldn't even speak properly. Cursing himself, he gave her a hurried glance and went. Not a moment later, he heard the *husband* grumble and then his female make some soothing sounds. Ronin smacked his head, realizing that he had been rude, and he turned around to say 'thank you' to the couple. He then gave the *oh-so beautiful* fullhuman female a final yearning look and left.

Presently, Ronin paused and thought, *Damn! I wish there were a way to know that young female. Perhaps I can come back later...but what would I say to her?* And he berated himself for thinking he could come here and meet a girl, not knowing anything about Downside society, nor even anything about initiating a conversation with an unconnected person. When he started again, he threw all frustrating thoughts aside and walked with his mind totally focused on the package, which he continued to hold with growing eagerness.

He *knew* no one would believe him when he told them what he had done during their next diginection. Ronin? Go Downside? And with courage enough to ask for realmeat? But he had done it! He had done it and done it *all* on his own! Except–but he stopped that thought before it discombobulated him again.

Now, he needed to find a quiet place where he could sit and savor his food. He had no idea what animal had been sacrificed to provide the substance for the sandwich, but it must be from one of the few large animal species that still existed on the planet. His friend had told him that it was probably raven meat.

Ronin searched for a while to find a spot away from anyone, because the Downside mind map lacked the details it had for locations Upside, and being forced to use his eyes and memory to keep track of where he was going—so that he could get back to the Connection Port later that day—was causing him great distress. He understood now why his friends had said that they never explored anything beyond the city center.

The trial and error process, which caused him to engage into decrepit streets and unadvisable impasses, none of which led to any park or quiet area where he could eat his sandwich, was tightening his chest quite horribly and giving him nervous sweats. *What if I can't find my way back? What if I get lost in here? Why can't I find all these large parks that are supposed to be around here???*

Some ten more minutes later, he came to a large intersection with four streets going off in different directions and he started to panic. He paused, took five deep breaths and when his pulse slowed, he decided to make his way back to an earlier intersection. He struggled two long minutes to remember the way, but he did eventually, and got there a short while later.

Finding his way back to this one location he remembered relieved him greatly, and he now looked more carefully at the layout of this part of the city to try and find the park his mind map said should be around here. After spending another minute comparing what he saw with what he remembered having already explored—which was a feat in and of itself, as people Upside never had to remember how to get somewhere given that their mind maps or the autonomous vehicles took them everywhere—he picked the road on the right and got going, promising himself to return to Connection Port if he failed again, and the hell with his meal!

But he did finally find the park he was looking for, and quickly spied a bench set in the middle of a small clearing of the park. He walked to it, speeding-up his step a little, so eager he was to get his teeth into the sandwich and forget about the thirty, stressful minutes he had just spent getting there.

Ronin sat himself down on the weathered bench, and looked around to make certain no one was close enough to see him unwrap his food. As the strange fiber wrapping came off, he sensed his mouth starting to salivate. He also felt nervous and anxious, afraid that anyone who saw him would immediately recognize him for an Upsider and know what he was doing. He berated himself for it, but what could he do? This place was as foreign to him as Kepler or Enceladus given that he had only ever been Upside, even when he travelled.

The sandwich that he saw under the wrapping looked simply marvelous, so marvelous that all the glands in his mouth started watering uncontrollably. People of the past would have said 'divine,' but using such ancient terms was frowned upon Upside, and a person could only read them in antique digirecords, or in books—if one let themself give-in to a sudden desire to visit the *library*, a facility in New Rome that kept records from before the cybernetic age.

The smell now thoroughly enveloped him, and he closed his eyes while he breathed it in. He let himself feel the shivers that ran through him. Nothing he knew Upside compared to this; nothing he had ever tasted, smelled, or looked at. The food there was as synthetic as their bodies, their speech, their relations, and everything else. Only the organic parts on a shrinking portion of Upsiders still had anything in common with people down here.

Having given one more suspicious look around, Ronin brought the sandwich to his mouth and bit into it. His entire body exploded with an onrush of sensations he had never felt before, not even during his visiloves. Some people said fleshlove was better, the best thing a human being could experience. But how would he know? Even though he still had a mostly organic body–including his head, torso, abdomen, *and* his reproductive organs–copulation was frowned upon Upside, and he was not one to go against the norms. Perhaps, he thought, if he could meet a fullhuman female Downside, he'd be able to know the truth of it since people down here came together as nature had originally intended it– experiencing sex in each other's presence. He thought of the young female he'd seen at the ricemeat vendor's booth, and sighed just as the taste and smell of the food in his mouth called his attention back with a bang, and he savored the realmeat, proud of himself for having had the courage to come down, purchase it, and eat it.

After Ronin finished swallowing his first bite and had licked his lips completely, he brought up his hands to get a new bite, all the while enjoying the smell of it when the sound of a male, coming from behind, caused him to freeze.

"What'you downing there?"

Ronin started, and quickly rewrapped his sandwich. He then looked-up with what he hoped was a "stay-away-from-me" look on his face and inadvertently sent a reply via his brainchip. The male, of course, didn't receive him.

Damn! Did I just do that? Ronin sighed, thought of a simple reply, and forced words through his voicebox again, "I'm *down* here…enjoying sun. Please, move along." Ronin didn't hate Downsiders–he just didn't know them–but not being able to properly converse with them made him extremely uncomfortable even though they should be the ones looking down before addressing him.

As it happened, *this* Downsider looked at him straight in the eye and asked again his question. Ronin forced himself to relax his jaw and said, "Please move along. I–just go." *Damn! That's not what I wanted to say. It's so frustrating! How do the others do it that come down here?*

The male, who must be very poor if his tattered clothes and dirty face and hands were any indication, looked at Ronin as if Ronin had said something funny. Ronin tried to shoo him away again, but the male must have completely misunderstood him because he came to sit next to him instead.

He said, "I cn tell you ain't from downere."

When Ronin blinked, the male repeated himself, but tried to speak more clearly and slowly this time, "I can tell you ain't not from Downside. I'nt asked what'ure doing here, but what'ure eatin' there."

Ronin cringed as he realized that the conversation with this vagrant was not going to end soon, and that he was going to be forced to struggle to understand and to speak. He took another moment to think about a reply that might end the conversation and said, "I…right. I am not…I am from Upside. But, I have to go, and I need to finish this before I do. Please go."

Ronin was surprised to understand the first part of the stranger's reply when it came, but he did not understand the second. The man said, "Well, if you're gonna be a jerk, then I *will* go. Buhaps you can give abit what'you got 'fore."

When Ronin stared at him blankly, the male sighed and left, making obscene motions, grumbling and cursing. Ronin didn't know *what* the obscenities might be, but he knew their intent. He felt bad for the male, and if he hadn't been so anxious to be done with the conversation, he might have given him some credits. But who knew if the male even had a fingerchip.

Ronin waited a while before returning his attention to his sandwich. By then, it had grown a little cold, and he was no longer overpowered by its smell, though it still looked deliciously appetizing. *I need to learn to use my voice if I want to come back. In fact, I want to come back! But who can I even practice with? They will all think me weird, and it's not like any of my friends are any better at it than I am. Except for Canyon, but he wouldn't care to teach me. Or maybe I should just put money aside, so I can have an electronic voicebox implanted in me–that way it won't be so hard speaking my thoughts. But it'll take me months to have enough money for* that*!*

Ronin sighed, looked down at his hand, gave a look around to be sure the poor male had left and that no one else was coming this way, and finally unwrapped the sandwich again and hurried to finish it.

It did not take Ronin long to realize that realmeat could not be swallowed so fast when he almost choked on a bite. At that moment, a sound came from behind and he turned his head nervously. What he saw caused him to accidentally swallow a large chunk and he choked again, this time badly, and he felt like he was going to die.

It was the young Downsider female! What was she doing here?! She approached him, and he turned away, embarrassed, all the while hacking furiously. Irritatingly, she moved to his other side to face him. Ronin would have cursed if he could have, but when he saw a bottle of water in front of his eyes, he took it without a second thought. After several small gulps of water, the bolus finally passed into his stomach, and Ronin breathed with relief. He thanked the young female with a smile still shy, but honestly grateful. He said, "Did–Why–I mean–How did you–"

The female said, "I've seen it happen before to other Upsiders. Maybe you're not used to very chewy foods anymore."

Ronin raised a questioning eyebrow, and the girl continued, "Anyways, I went home with my pa after you left, and on our way, we came by some people who were talking excitedly about an Upsider they saw going through the neighborhood and seemed to be looking for a park. We understood that this must be you. When we got home, I asked my pa if I could bring you a bottle, and he let me come find you—to avoid any trouble in case you choked on the sandwich."

"Your…pa?"

"Yes, my father."

Ronin nodded and with a voice still raspy said, "You're not as…difficult to understand."

The girl smiled and said, "I found books, and then I found more, and I studied. And then my uncle let me use his visiontab to learn while listening."

"An….uncle? You mean–"

"My pa's brother."

"Right."

The girl did not say anything and waited instead for Ronin to speak again. But Ronin watched the girl for a moment, enraptured by her strange beauty and awed by her simplicity. Then, he said, "You…don't…distrust me."

The girl gave him a gentle smile, said, "No, I know Upsiders are not all jerks."

"Jerks?"

"Mean."

Ronin nodded.

The girl said, "You're not used to talking."

"No…I'm not. It is…it's difficult for me. We rarely use our voices Upside."

The girl smiled again, while shaking her head in disbelief. She then looked up at him and said, timidly, "I wish I could visit Upside someday. But it'd probably be worse for me; I don't think they like Downsiders up there."

Ronin made a small frown at that which he quickly replaced with a smile. He was truly enjoying the girl's spoken words; they were soothing, and they were the only things he received from her, as opposed to the invasive thoughts people sent each other Upside.

Looking at the girl with great curiosity, he now asked, "How did you…find me?"

The girl's reply, which she gave with great amusement, surprised Ronin, "I just asked if anyone had seen you, and since you are quite…conspicuous, many people did. They told me where you went, and I followed."

"Do you have a mind map?"

"A…*mind map*? No, unless you mean my memory."

Ronin was truly startled to hear that people down here could find their way so easily. Would they find it as easy Upside?

He said, "It was…stressful. Stressful for me to have to find my—"

A challenge suddenly invaded Ronin's mind. *"Ronin Clareborn. Do you need assistance?"*

It was the sending of a Control cop. Ronin started. Seeing this, the girl turned and almost jumped out of her skin when her eyes landed on the cop.

Ronin took a quiet breath, turned toward the cop as well and said aloud, "Yes, officer?"

The cop, a nongendered human, said in a slightly irritating metallic voice, "Mr. Ronin Clareborn, Upsiders may explore, but they may not fraternize with plains people. I assume the fullhuman female is here to assist you with something."

The cop appeared to want to be lenient with Ronin and was suggesting to him a way out of the bind he might find himself in if he gave the wrong answer. But he also seemed to want to give the Downsider a warning by speaking aloud.

Ronin thought quickly and was surprised when a reply that would keep him out of trouble came to him. He sent, *"I am sorry, officer. I choked on a piece of the wrapping, and the fullhuman, who was passing by, gave me the bottle of water."*

The girl watched anxiously, wondering what the boy, whose name she now knew was Ronin, was saying to the cop.

The cop narrowed the fleshy lids around his synthetic eyes and looked suspiciously at the wrapping Ronin held.

Ronin controlled his heart rate, to keep it even. If he let it speed up, the cop would know he was hiding something. Ronin might not have many special skills, but he did know how to control his reactions–most of the time.

The cop seemed satisfied that the wrapping held nothing illicit and said, looking at the female, "Was the bottle previously opened?"

The girl replied at once, "No! It's a clean, new bottle. I saw the man in trouble, and I came to give it to him, officer."

Forcing words out of his still unpracticed throat, Ronin said, "That is the truth, officer. She was…only here to help." Then, turning to the girl, he said, "You can go now. I am fine." Ronin felt an immediate pang of guilt and saw such a sadness in the female's eyes, as she moved to go, that he couldn't help adding, "Thank you," even if it made the cop frown.

The girl gave him a sad smile back and left at once. Ronin wondered if she would look back, but she did not, though she did pause a moment before engaging on the park's trail and disappearing under the trees.

The cop, too, left after making certain that Ronin had understood he was not to fraternize with the locals anymore.

Ronin put a hand to his forehead and took a deep breath. As he did, thoughts of the girl invaded his mind. And he let them run freely for a while. He found the thoughts of seeing the girl again, spending more time with her…exciting, in a way he had never felt before. Her voice, her smile—the quietness of them. Were all fullhuman females like that? But his excitement was quashed when he reminded himself that he could barely string two spoken words together. Canyon would probably say, 'So what? You don't need words to enjoy fleshlove.' The thing was, that was *not at all* what he wanted right now, and in any case, he hated the thought of sharing his body with a fullhuman female as if with a synthetic. No, what he desired was her…her company, her presence.

But now that the Control cop suspected him, he knew he couldn't be found with the girl again, and he sighed deeply and cursed in his mind for a long while as he summoned various scenarios that would enable him to return here and get to know the girl. In the end, he concluded frustratingly that there *was* nothing he could do, *except to get away from* effin! *Earth; from its unnatural ways and illogical injunctions against the true human nature*. As he thought about it more, he realized that Earth's leaders could not even understand him given that they all had mostly synthetic bodies.

His only option was to leave, but how? . His chest fluttered with apprehension when he realized that the only quick way out was with the Empress's Army, who had contacted him recently, to recruit him. But he hated violence more than Upside's backwards ways. Why would he join? He felt a small surge of excitement take him as he remembered something. *I can join as an Ordnance officer! I have the required education after all, and they'll outfit me with all the latest communications technology.* Indeed, through one of his friends who had joined the army the year before, he had learned that all officers whose function required interaction with the inhabitants of the Empire's colonies were 'equipped' with electronic voice boxes. *Yes, I'd then be able to meet, and actually* converse, *with a fullhuman girl like the sandy-haired girl who saved me…and whose name…I'd like to know.*

Effin' Tec! I thought it was Earth's government or just Upside society that was driving us away from our nature. But no! it's Tec itself, propagating like a virus."

Ronin was sending to Dovard, his bunkmate. Ronin had finally found his way into the Empress's Army and had now been deployed to his third assignment, this one to help implement the new Ordnance Management system on Enceladus. He soon understood though, that even on Earth's galactic colonies, where the majority of the inhabitants were still fullhuman, the trend toward Tec integration was pervasive and just as powerfully appealing to them as it had been to Upside Earthers a thousand years before. The realization was deeply disappointing to him, and he had spent days lamenting the situation, wondering why it was, and asking himself, his friends, and his mentors what force continued to drive humans so relentlessly toward their own erasure. And no one had been able to provide him with an acceptable answer. Most actually thought him strange to complain about what had liberated humanity from nature.

He thought: *At least, I've gotten one thing out of this.* And indeed, he had, although what had enabled him to finally converse with the girl from Earth like a normal human being was the Tec the army had implanted in his throat. Ronin groaned and kicked his bed's railing at the thought of the contradiction.

Dovard, a frustrating fatalist who saw the evolution of humanity as a preordained necessity, replied with a metallic voice, "Humans have complained about Tec for as long as it has existed, Ronin. And its development has never slowed, except during the great depressions. No one will willingly eliminate Tec or willingly reduce its capabilities and uses. Our intelligence itself creates novel challenges and threats which can only be overcome with new things that it must then create, generating a vicious circle we can't get out of. Tec is one of these things."

Ronin sighed, annoyed, and then said aloud with his own metallic voice, "Yes, you've told me that before, Dov."

After three months of intense training, spent thinking thoughts and speaking them, from simple to more and more complex, Ronin could finally express himself decently through sound, though the ubiquitous use of mind-to-mind messaging in official, as well as in personal communications, constantly threatened his new-found ability. What was more, he was still not used to his synthetic voice. The medbots had done their best to match his natural voice with his internal voice, but their attempts had been mediocre to say the least. "I'm thinking of joining Proconsul Genghis's mission to Kepler. Have you heard about it?"

"No."

Continuing with his e-voicebox, but speaking quietly—conspiratorially—Ronin said, "Karo and Yary told me that the general actually intends to go to K'Tara."

"K'Tara?"

Ronin did not immediately reply, but instead—feeling an annoying pain in his back as he repositioned himself on his bunk—sent Dovard a complaint about the bunk's discomfort. Indeed, troops with bodies that required *horizontal* rest were forced to use the most uncomfortable cots for beds, and if they complained to a quartermaster, they were scorned for being a *lessthan*, meaning *less than a fully enhanced human*. Ronin often wondered if *fullsynths* were even human, but they still laughed and cried and got angry—and they had organic brains—, so perhaps they were—perhaps.

After releasing a loud groan and cursing at the bed, he said, "It's one of the outer planets, one of the earliest ones to have been inseminated, but still unsettled by present-day Earthers."

Dovard swiveled on his bed and looked down toward Ronin with squinting, questioning eyes.

Ronin switched to mind-to-mind communication and sent, *"It appears the general and his followers want to go there because they're fed-up with their mechanical bodies and want to...well...be able to finish their years as fullhumans."*

Dovard yelled an incredulous, "What!?"

"I know it sounds crazy, Dov, but there are a *lot* of fullsynths who'd like nothing more than to transfer their brains back into an organic body."

"That is not my point, Ronin. How would they even *obtain* organic bodies if they went to this…K'Tara?"

"Karo and Yary said the K'Tarans' culture will enable the general to obtain the bodies of recently deceased fullhumans. He will bring robodocs there, ready to perform the brain-transfer operation. Surgeons used to do that kind of procedure before the prohibition against cloning, and robodocs can apparently replicate it perfectly."

This time, Dovard switched to mind-to-mind communication, *"It still sounds crazy, Ronin. It sounds crazy and backward. And it also sounds like an unsanctioned mission. Are you sure you heard right?"*

"Am I sure? Of course, I am! Karo and Yary told me during a diginection a month ago, and they've told me more about it each time we've connected since; they didn't say anything about the mission being unsanctioned. Perhaps the Empress is letting the general do it because she knows he is unsatisfied with our way of life, as are a lot of other people too. So, this may be her way of getting rid of a problem before it threatens the order she has worked so hard to establish."

Dovard made a grimace and said, "And you want to join them to go live among stone-age fullhumans?"

Ronin frowned at his friend's insult but nodded seriously and then said, "I think you should join too."

Dovard's face scrunched itself into an ugly form unlike that of his perfect body. "Why would I do that? And join what? A secret mission to an unknown planet, just so that the general and his lot may shed their mechanical bodies?"

Ronin bobbed his head left to right.

Dovard jumped down from his bunk with the skill of a cat, then sat himself in a chair—another uncomfortable piece of furniture for the quarters of the lessthans which invariably knotted Ronin's back muscles. But Dovard did not mind the metallic seat.

Now, his friend stretched his legs, crossed his arms and said, "I still don't see why you would want to go there, anyway. And I thought you wanted to try and bring the fullhuman girl Upside, to the Disk…to have her as your companion. Though I don't know *how* you would do that and what you find appealing in fleshlove."

Ronin blinked several times and snorted with an expression of revulsion on his face as he realized what his friend was saying. "What are you talking about? She's not some synthetic for someone to have; what's more, I haven't even tried it yet. But how would *you* know what fleshlove is, anyway?"

"Trust me, *I know*. But you haven't answered my question."

Ronin looked at his bunkmate curiously. Unable to decide from his expression whether Dovard had actually experienced fleshlove or whether he was making a cynical comment, and seeing his friend's insistent stare, Ronin sighed and said, "I do have something going with Julia—we connect every few days for a couple of hours, during your longshift, through an old videochat system to talk—" Dovard raised a surprised brow, "and I *do* want to get Julia away from Earth, but where would I take her? From what I've seen, the colonized planets are just as bad as Earth, and all are moving toward greater and greater Tec Integration."

Dovard now bobbed his head. Ronin was right as far as the general trend was concerned. There was only one planet he knew of that explicitly forbade all Tec. But then, the people there were most unwelcoming of outsiders, unless they were one of the faithful lost—and his friend wasn't one.

Ronin continued, "When Karo and Yary told me about K'Tara, I got really excited, and I scoured the records for whatever information may be available on it. As you might guess, there wasn't much to be found—at least not where I looked—but the few old records I found describe the planet as having already had a thriving biosphere with sentient lifeforms when the seeding pod arrived there in 2181. There are even fewer records of the planet's condition since then, but the ones I found indicate that the seeds placed there have given rise to a flourishing human civilization. One also states that no modern Earthers have yet established themselves there; it's just too remote. So, if there is one place where I could take Julia, perhaps that is it."

This time, Dovard chuckled and said, "Knowing how anti-Tec you are, I can see the appeal of a planet like K'Tara." Then, with his usual contradictory tone, he added, "But, I still don't know why you would take this girl with you; digimates are much less trouble. And I thought you had one yourself; didn't it give you the loving and companionship you needed?"

Ronin sighed, annoyed by his friend's insistence on questioning his motives. He said, "I didn't use my digimate that way. I just used Bali to take care of things for me, so I could focus on my studies."

Dovard cocked his brows, said, "You are a strange one, Ronin. That's granted." Then he continued to annoy Ronin with his thoughts and theories about human relationships, speckled with historical references showing how unhappy humans were when they reproduced through copulation and sought the satisfaction of their emotional needs in other humans. He told him also that even the eventual acceptance of non-standard gender and sexual relationships didn't increase their happiness. No, digilove was the best thing to happen to humans since the beginning of time.

In the end, Ronin just grumbled and said, "Whatever Dov, but it's just not how I feel when I'm with Julia."

Dovard shrugged his shoulders, and Ronin asked, "So, will you join the Proconsul's unit with me? Because even if you don't care how you love, or how we continue to be dehumanized, I'm certain you won't find another civilization like the one on K'Tara anywhere else in the galaxy, and you *will* want to study that."

Indeed, Dovard had joined the Ordnance Section of the Imperial Army six months ago to explore the galaxy, as had Ronin. But Dovard's desire to explore was motivated by a wish to learn the changing ways and mores of humanity as it spread across the galaxy, whereas Ronin's desire had a more reactionary motivation: that of getting away from what he considered the unnatural ways of Upside Earthers; of finding a better planet to live on.

"You make a good point there, Ronin,"

Feeling hopeful for the first time since the start of their conversation, Ronin's question rushed from his synthetic voicebox with a squeak, "So, you'll consider it?!"

"I will…if it is an approved mission."

Ronin gleamed and told Dovard he'd get the answer to his question, after which he laid back on his cot, and just smiled, excited, satisfied.

As for Dovard, he got up and stripped to change into his uniform to get ready for his next shift while telling Ronin, as he often did while changing, about another captivating story he had started reading, this one concerning the Roman emperor Marcus Aurelius, and which he strongly recommended his comrade should read too.

Ronin listened with half an ear and glanced at his friend every so often. Dovard's upper body, which was unenhanced, was that of an athletic person, slim and muscular. Indeed, even though he was an intellectual, which was a little unusual for the army, he very much enjoyed climbing walls of all sorts on the various planets where they were posted or which they visited during their leaves. His chest, like his face, was hairless, as were the bodies of most humans since the beginning of the Cybernetic Age. His bottom half, on the other hand, was completely mechanical but looked just like his top with its matched *synthetic flesh* covering.

Seeing his friend 'naked' did not bother Ronin, except for the fact that—like most enhanced humans, who preferred not to be burdened by sexual organs, especially since reproduction was strictly artificial since before the Cybernetic Age, and loving was essentially achieved virtually, whether between two persons or between a person and a synthetic linked through the Connection—Dovard did not have any genitals either, except for the synthetic organ necessary to the elimination of urine, and this still made Ronin uncomfortably self-conscious, and he could not help questioning himself each time, then berating and telling himself that it was the rest of humanity that was strange.

After Dovard left, Ronin continued to think about Proconsul Genghis's mission to K'Tara—even if it was possible that it was unsanctioned, as Dovard said, though he hoped it wasn't, so that his all-too-principled friend would join too. Those reflections were suddenly replaced by thoughts of Julia, the fullhuman female he had met Downside ten months back, and whom he had visited several times following that first encounter despite having been warned by a cop not to have contact with the girl again. But Ronin had been unable to resist the need to know the fullhuman girl, and his friend Canyon had provided him with a fake ID so that he might return Downside without being caught, so long as he didn't come across the Control cop who had surprised him with the girl on that first visit. So, Ronin had returned, and he soon developed intense, surprising, and extremely pleasurable feelings for Julia. He became unable to resist the need for her conversation and for the sensations he felt when he was with her.

Just now, he recalled one of his encounters with the sandy-haired girl. The memory was there in his mind in complete fullness, with visual, auditory, olfactory and tactile impressions.

The memory was of his fourth visit Downside, the time during which they had touched. Ronin arrived at their usual meeting place, in the ancient city of Boulder, at precisely

15:00 on that day, the time of their appointment. Indeed, he no longer felt the need or desire to explore Downside on his own and much preferred visiting places he hadn't yet seen with Julia by his side. By then, her father—Ronin didn't understand why only the father cared what she did with him and not the mother, especially since mothers invested so much more in their progeny than their husbands did—had learned and accepted that they were seeing each other, and he had allowed his daughter to spend more time with him, though never later than 22:00, which was another thing he still did not understand though Julia had tried to explain the reasons to him.

When he saw Julia approach that day, his breath caught, and his body reacted with swelling and flushing. Julia wore a piece of garment, which was wide and open at the bottom, called a skirt, and the skirt showed her legs in a way he had never seen Upside, and it sent his heart racing, while her top was covered by a sleeveless shirt which left bare her graceful, smooth, tan arms. Julia noticed his reaction, and she lowered her eyes as a shy smile appeared on her beautiful lips. Once both recovered from the unexpected experience, Julia took him to the local botanical gardens, where they spent the rest of the afternoon walking, stopping, smelling, and smiling.

Compared to the rest of Boulder, or to the rest of the planet's surface for that matter, the gardens were incredibly lush and alive; it was the Central Government's way of giving the Downsiders some measure of beauty to take their minds off their daily misery, going so far in its generosity as to make the gardens free. When Ronin sighed in front of a plant with vibrantly-colored and incredibly fragrant flowers, known as *lilac*, Julia smiled and…and touched his hand.

Ronin kept staring at the flowers, not knowing what to do, but he did not resist Julia's hand when it slid itself into his, and her fingers laced his. A new emotion overwhelmed his senses, and he did not turn toward her, afraid that if he did and she smiled at him, he wouldn't know how to react. So, he simply squeezed her hand, the moment passed, and they continued their walk through the gardens.

Their conversations had become slightly more fluid by now, with Ronin's mastery of spoken language having grown steadily over the course of their encounters. And he felt intensely grateful to Julia who seemed to genuinely enjoy showing him how to sound the words she knew he must be thinking, which always surprised him. By the end of their walk through the gardens, Ronin was feeling quite satisfied, proud even, when—as he admired the plants near the exit— he said in a long and almost perfect sentence, "This must be the most beautiful plant of them all, and…they must…do it on purpose, to leave the memory of the gardens in our minds before we return to our homes or…" His tongue tied itself trying to say, "wherever else." Julia smiled another smile which flushed his skin with a warm sensation.

After leaving the gardens, Julia took them to her family's shop to get something that she had prepared for him since she had not brought him anything on this day, as she had on their two previous encounters. Indeed, on his second visit, Julia had brought him another *realmeat* sandwich, but different from the one he had purchased for himself the first time. This one had been even more enjoyable, sending an explosion of flavors exciting different parts of his mouth as he bit, chewed, and then swallowed it. Julia had called it a *carnita* sandwich. But some unexpected passerby had almost caught them with it, and so, Ronin had decided that he no longer wished to take silly risks, and, on their third encounter, she had brought him a soupy vegetable dish instead, one called *chili*. He remembered not liking this very much; perhaps it was one of the vegetables—the beans—which had a strange texture he disliked.

Presently, Ronin waited in front of the shop, blushing and feeling awkward under Julia's father's stares, her mother's smiles, and her sisters' giggles. He tried to say something to them, hoping to shift their focus, so he told them about the beauty of the gardens. But his words came out rather clumsily, and her father narrowed his brows, as if wondering whether his daughter's companion was an idiot, while the mother and the sisters redoubled on their smiles and giggles.

Ronin was relieved when Julia finally came back out, holding a thermal container. But he did not relax until they had left and walked back to the spot they used as their meeting place, a busy plaza with restaurants and bars, and a place she told him was called a *theater*, where they showed movies on a large screen. They had chosen this place because of the crowd which would make them less noticeable to any Control cop, but also because it was on the north side of town, opposite the side patrolled by the cop that had warned him on his first visit.

Once seated on their usual bench which seemed to always be available, Julia smiled with a childish excitement as she took out spoons, opened the thermal, and finally invited him to try the soup.

The broth's fragrance made Ronin close his eyes and breathe in the warm vapor. When he finally took a spoonful of it under Julia's expectant stare, his taste buds exploded! The *pozole*—that was the name of the soup—was just as divine as the realmeat had been. The soup contained flavors which were totally new to him, despite the galactic database of synthetic foods served Upside.

When they finished the soup, Ronin thanked his good luck, and then thanked Julia, with the sincerest smile— followed by a sudden sense of guilt. Julia asked why the frown, and after a short moment of frustration to put the words together, he told her that he felt guilty for never having anything to share with her. Julia tried to convince him that she did not mind, but Ronin would not be convinced, and so he decided to take a risk. He said, "You…told me that…that you wished you could see the movie…the movie that's playing there tonight. I want to take you to see it."

Julia was ecstatic then uncertain. She did not wish him to get into trouble for her. But Ronin insisted; it was right that he should do something in return since he could not bring her Upside, nor bring anything for her when he visited. And anyway, he was curious about this ancient technology which they used to show movies to a large group of people in the same room. So, they went.

Ronin could feel Julia fidgeting anxiously next to him. When they got to the ticket counter, and he touched his finger to the scanner to pay, and then the attendant asked Julia for *her* finger to record her attendance, Ronin hoped—no, prayed to the Empress—that the Control cops would not be alerted by the association of the two chips. He sighed with relief when nothing happened. It seemed they were okay.

The experience of the movie-on-a-screen certainly felt peculiar to Ronin. When viewing a movie Upside, he was always *in* the action, but here, he was *outside* of it, experiencing something external to himself, as if spying on other people's doings, or as if watching ships come and go, or watching spacewalkers making repairs to a ship from an Upside observation deck.

The movie was not about a topic ever presented Upside either; it was about a male and a female caught in the middle of a disastrous storm following the failure of the weather control system, the male and the female saving each other and finally…falling in love. Ronin was utterly fascinated by the evolution of the relationship between the two main characters, and he wondered whether the same thing was happening between him and Julia.

Somewhere near the middle of the movie, when the protagonists started to become emotionally attached to each other, Julia took his hand and began squeezing it every so often in reaction to some frightful event, until she eventually grabbed his entire arm. But though the public display of physical contact—even in the dimly lit room—made him uncomfortable, he could not prevent his body's reactions which went from simple but deep inhalations to sudden quickenings of his pulse and finally to shivers.

And those reactions were nothing compared to what happened to him when, at the end of the movie, the male and female embraced and…loved each other. Indeed, the scene caused Julia to lift her head from his chest, turn her face up, and kiss him. It was exhilarating—the touch of human lips against human lips. His entire body erupted then, and every caress, every squeeze of Julia's hands on his neck or face or legs roused him like nothing he had ever known before. And he felt something else too: a sense of belonging, of…of wanting to belong…and of wan—

Just at that moment, as if they had been waiting for the end of the movie to enter, the Control cops rushed in and put their cold, unyielding hands on Ronin's and Julia's shoulders.

Ronin shook himself out of the memory which still angered him. Firstly because of the way the Control cops had treated Julia—like a criminal, and secondly because before they took her away, he was not even allowed to say goodbye. But he was glad for one thing: the same cop who had caught him with Julia, when she came to save him in the park, had spoken in his favor, saying that he was only a misguided youth, when the Control chief had considered revoking his passport for illegal proximity and—especially—for Ronin's "malfunctioning" monitoring chip. The chief had, therefore, let him keep his papers, with the understanding that the next time they found him here with the girl, she would be jailed, and his passport would be revoked at once.

Keeping his passport had been a great relief to him, or his dreams—all of them—would have been quashed, and he would have been forced to spend the rest of his life living Upside, a place he despised. But there had been another consequence to his 'offense', which his pleas had not succeeded in preventing; he had been forced to undergo the most humiliating physical exam before returning Upside to ensure he was not bringing back any dangerous infection. And the fact that it had been performed by a robodoc did not embarrass him any less.

Ronin had spent several days, after returning Upside, bemoaning his situation, wondering about Julia, and being unproductive and causing his employer—Upside Logistics— to warn him that unless he got his numbers back on track at once, there would be consequences. But Canyon had come through for him again and found a way for him and Julia to connect through some non-monitored communications system.

Ronin now remembered Julia's frightened face when they had their first connection, and she told him of the fine the authorities had imposed on her father for her transgression, and of his subsequent rage and disappointment. This had only made things worse for Ronin, but he was able to assuage Julia's father when Canyon agreed to do him one final favor by finding a way to replace the man's credits.

Ever since that day, Ronin and Julia had remained in communication, connecting every so often, when his schedule allowed it. Each time, they began with Ronin telling Julia how much he missed her, and she telling him how silly he was. Then, they spent some time talking of their most recent excitements or frustrations, and they invariably ended their connections with a promise from Ronin to find a way to bring her to him, and a promise of eternal love from her. Eternal love. He didn't even know what love was. Was that what he was feeling?

A comm alert rang in Ronin's mind just then; it was a visual notification from the Staffing Office. With his breath catching, and his heart palpitating, Ronin sent the alert to the wallscreen—and he yelled.

It was with incredible, suppressed, elation that Ronin walked toward the Off-worlder section of the Disk's First Level this morning—with Julia at his side to go find some clothes for her. *Julia.* He still could not believe he had found a way for her to join the General's mission to K'Tara. Everyone had told him that the Government rarely allowed a Downsider to come Upside, let alone allowed one to relocate or join their military. But he had done it!

He had suggested the idea to Julia a couple of months after they started on the strange relationship, a relationship which he could not live without and which none of his friends understood yet, except perhaps for Canyon. A few were even repulsed by the idea of an intimate relationship with another person. Ronin did not care. He could not hide his repeated visits Downside nor—after a while—the reason for them, but he did not discuss his growing feelings or plans for Julia either; only Canyon and Dovard knew of them.

When Ronin first told Julia about his idea of them joining a mission that General Genghis was planning for next year, her head had pulled back with shock and incomprehension. What did he mean? Why would she join a military mission, and how could she when she was a mere civilian and a

Downsider on top of it? And what was the mission? How would she fit in, even if she *could* join? And for what purpose? And wasn't it possible that they might be killed? And…

Ronin had quietly explained that the risk was low, and then explained the general's real goal. He told her that this was the only way for them to be able to live together as they wanted to.

After a few weeks of researching things, including life on other planets, military roles for civilians, the risks of modern warfare, and reading whatever she could find on the proconsul himself, she knew that Ronin was probably right. Still, she asked him why they couldn't simply move to one of the closer colonies, such as the one on Enceladus? When he replied that he did not wish to live in a colony where they would be forced to enhance their bodies with Tec, she agreed to his plan, though she remained apprehensive. But she loved him, and she knew he loved her more than anyone else she had ever dated, though he was an Upsider. So, she would trust him. All that was left was to convince her family—and for Ronin to get her admitted on the mission, which he accomplished surprisingly easily.

Her family, however, had been divided about it. Her mother, who had always trusted him more than her father, reacted with a joyous smile after her initial tears, which she had cried more for the knowledge that she might never see her daughter again, than for any concern about her safety; she knew Ronin had put himself at great risk to pursue her daughter, and that he would therefore take care of Julia, no matter what obstacles lay ahead of them. And if joining him in this adventure was Julia's road to a better future, Mercedes would not oppose it.

Julia's father, on the other hand, had refused to discuss her decision for several days as he grappled with his beliefs—and fears—that she would become as disconnected from true life as the Upsiders; that she might even become a *robot*. But, after doing his best to convince himself that his daughter would turn badly, he was unable to do so without finding himself ridicule. So, when the day came for her departure, he went to see her as she fretfully gathered her papers to go to the local Emigration Office with Ronin, to be allowed to leave Downside.

There, in the living room—with everyone watching anxiously—Ronin heard the man speak to his daughter in a way no one had ever spoken to him, Upside. And when Julia's father was done saying what he had wanted to say, and Julia had hugged him the way she always did, while promising him that she would remain the daughter he had always known, the burly man showed his acceptance through the tears he let flow.

Now, as they crossed a large plaza surrounded by restaurants and shops, something tugged at Ronin. He glanced at Julia, and his smile faded when he saw her fearful and confused. It seemed that, as excited as Julia had been before leaving Downside that morning, the unfamiliarity of everything was beginning to scare her. He wanted to take her hand, squeeze it, to tell her it would be okay, but he could not; she was supposed to be someone he had met by chance on one of his trips Downside and whom he had recognized as a resource the General could use on his mission because of her skills in natural language. So, he gave her sidelong glances every so often and tried to encourage her with tender smiles as they made their way to their destination.

To Julia, this place—*Upside*—was like something out of a person's imagination. It frightened her because of its people—if they were even people—and because of its sheer eeriness, suspended as it was in the upper atmosphere. But seeing Upsiders down below, on the planet, had never caused her such anxiety because, there, she was home and *they* were the foreigners.

Here, she was out of her element. No one spoke a word and they did not look at each other, even when she knew they must be communicating, such as when she and Ronin were at the Immigration Office for her to be admitted, and Ronin stood in front of the Immigration Officer's desk to hand her papers to the man, answer questions *for* her, take a tablet from the officer, and then passed it to her to sign some electronic forms. Not a word had been exchanged between Ronin and the officer, and the only time the man spoke to her was to ask, in a harsh metallic voice, if she swore to all the statements on the tablet.

The only other sounds she did hear, since arriving Upside, were those of doors opening and closing to let vehicles and people in or out of different buildings; the whirring noises of the vehicles slowing down to land somewhere; the clip clopping of feet; the friction of the rolling mats taking people here and there; and the clicking sounds of the objects that people carried on them.

But despite the strangeness of it all, some things *did* amaze and please her, such as the "clothing store" where a machine—there were several such machines all around the otherwise empty room—scanned her from all sides and ten minutes later spat out a perfectly-fitted replica of the Citizen's Suit she had chosen from the long list provided on the machine's screen. But the same experience also managed to frustrate and humiliate her. Indeed, when Julia placed her finger on the machine to pay for the merchandise, the computer rejected the payment, and Ronin was forced to call one of the rare clerks—without seeming to do so, of course. The person who came—a genderless person as was the case for most Upsiders—never even spoke to her but instead must have exchanged some thoughts with Ronin, after which it brusquely picked up her finger, scanned it again, and a moment later left the same way it had come, without a word. But Ronin's grunt and turn of the head told her that the person had sent another thought to him.

"Ey said you should get a brainchip implanted if you want to survive here."

"Ey?"

"We use different pronouns for genderless people."

"Oh."

Not a moment later, Julia noticed the clerk turning around to look straight at them for the first time. He—ey—seemed irate and resentful.

Anxiously, she whispered, "What happened?"

Ronin tried to contain a proud, bragging smile, "I told em to try and…fuck eirself. That made em very angry because, of course, ey can't."

Julia wanted to embrace Ronin, just then, though his words shocked her. But she gave him a warm, thankful and happy smile instead; no one had ever stood up for her like this. Still, it did not take away the sense of complete and utter alienation she felt since arriving on the Disk.

"It will get better," Ronin said quietly, "once we get on ship next week; most military personnel have electronic voiceboxes."

Julia's lips debated whether to turn up or down. In the end, her eyes said she wanted to trust him.

After changing into her new clothes, which felt like they fit her even better than the dresses Señora Ellora made for her in Boulder, Julia did not immediately step out of the changing room. Instead, she looked up and snorted at the reflection in the wall. Her eyes blinking, her lips moving left and then right, she said to herself: *I guess this is it; becoming one of them.* Julia exhaled a long and slow breath then stepped out of the changing booth.

She did so with a gulp and an anxious smile. Would Ronin like her new look? She asked him but Ronin did not say; he did not say anything. In fact, he seemed disappointed. When she asked him what was wrong, he shrugged and inhaled. When he exhaled, it was to whisper that as perfectly as the two-piece suit molded her body, she looked much better in her Downside dresses which showed her soft brown skin, and that he wished she did not need to transform herself into an Upsider.

Julia's brows pinched, but then she stared at him, insisting on knowing whether he liked the suit. Rolling his eyes, he said that she looked fine, and they left the shop.

Two long minutes later—long because the clothes forced her to walk with excessive self-consciousness—Julia heard Ronin indicate a large, ornate door to their right: The Grand Earth. A hotel that received common Off-worlders.

"Will you come in with me?"

"I can stay for a while but not overnight, nor can I accompany you to your room."

Her expression showed him she did not understand why that might be. He said, "People up here only meet in person in public areas or in offices, and only if a discussion or event cannot be held via diginection, such as for a meal or to exchange goods."

"Right." Julia exhaled in frustration then said with a slightly dispirited tone, "How long will we need to continue to lie, Ronin? I thought that, coming here, I'd be able to spend more time with you, without needing to hide from Control Cops."

Ronin shrugged his shoulders diffidently, then, seeing Julia's sincerely disheartened expression, he whispered, "At least until we are headed for K'Tara. General Genghis knows that the people going there with him are going so that they can live as we were meant to live, which includes being able to have a…a partner." Looking at her with an unusually intense gaze, he added, "I can do this…if you can."

Julia sighed, then smiled and said, "Okay."

Ronin followed Julia into the hotel, where he helped her check-in, which was done with minimal frustrations. When she commented on how welcoming the hotel's staff were and Ronin told her it was because they were just synthetics, Julia's first reaction was a questioning frown.

"Your father calls them robots, but they were also called androids before the cybernetic age."

Julia's eyes opened wide; she would not have known if he had not told her. When she realized she was staring at the bellbot—that's what Ronin had called the individual dressed as a bellboy—she thought, reactively, that it might get upset, but the thing just looked at her with a large, wide smile.

Julia scratched her head muttering something to herself.

Ronin, who had noticed her reaction said, "They can't get upset. They look like us, and can talk or send, but their emotions are limited to those pleasant ones. In fact, even the securitybots smile when they handle a…aghr! This is so frustrating. When they handle a recalcitrant citizen."

Ronin still had some difficulty speaking out loud fluently. It was not the pronunciation of the words that frustrated him—his electronic voicebox allowed him the most perfect enunciation. No, it was the *simple* process of translating his thoughts into words and sentences and then communicating them to his voicebox, so that the device might render them as sounds, that was irritatingly *unsimple*. Even though he had a rich and fluid imagery, an imagery combined with a vocabulary just as rich which he put to good use in mind-to-computer communications, he often found it difficult to draw upon the same vocabulary to render it through his voice.

Julia gave him a sympathetic grin, but quickly turned to look back at the bellbot, to check whether it was still smiling. However, something bothered her to think of the bot as a mere object, so she turned her head back toward Ronin with an expression that said how incredible all this felt to her, and followed him toward the restaurant at the back of the entry hall.

Julia was comforted to see that—here at least—using one's voice was not frowned upon. In fact, there were a few other guests doing the same. She supposed that they, too, were non-natives; probably from some other planet where Tec integration was not as advanced as it was Upside. But though they talked, they did so in the same hushed tones Ronin used, which meant that they were used to visiting here and knew the ways. This, too, gave her a frustrating sense of alienation.

Having sat down at a table near the window, Julia asked whether they would get menus, to which Ronin replied with a quizzical look.

"The selection is here." And Ronin tapped the pod sitting between them. A holographic projection of the restaurant's menu appeared. "You just need to touch your finger to the items you want."

Julia, unable to recognize what she was looking at, asked whether Ronin was going to order anything, to which he replied that his digimate had already sent his meal requirements to the restaurant. Julia puffed incredulously then asked if he would help her, and so, he did. They then waited for the food to arrive, mostly in silence, as she tried to make sense of this odd world. At least, when the food came, her nostrils opened with pleased anticipation. She did not recognize the foods on her plate, nor those on Ronin's, but they did smell good, and her primal senses dissipated her unease.

While they ate—and between the small bites she took of the unusually textured and flavored dishes Ronin had ordered—Julia questioned him about all sorts of things, most of which seemed to make Ronin uncomfortable. For instance, she asked him how to tell if a…an individual—she had no idea what word to use to refer to the different types since robots were not persons—was a human, a robot, a male or a female or something else. And she asked him if laws existed to protect the different types of individuals. Ronin answered all her questions patiently, though, it seemed, with some unease. Perhaps because he was afraid of doing so in a place where those spoken of might hear him. But, as Julia had noticed, no one was paying them any attention.

Ronin's answer to her question about distinguishing humans from robots was the oddest yet. He said, "Well, all of them do have a line on their nape showing where their cranium can be opened for servicing, but you can't always tell because of the hair. On the other hand, anyone with an unnatural skin color is definitely a human because synthetics have to have normal skin colors."

When she asked him with much surprise why robots—or rather, synthetics—wouldn't be forced to have a distinguishing color, Ronin shrugged, obviously embarrassed for not having an answer.

Having enjoyed and finished their dessert—a jelly-like, black spongy tort with speckles that looked like stars—Ronin paid for their meal, and they walked to the elevator. There, they said goodbye with quiet sighs, surreptitious touches of the hand, and business-like nods they forced themselves to give, with a promise from Ronin to pick her up the next morning at 08:00 to take her to the Military Processing Facility. As Julia started thanking him for his help all that day, Ronin stopped listening and froze—or so it seemed to her. In fact, he had reacted that way several times since they had arrived on the Disk, but she had never asked him about it. This time she did, and he replied with a slightly embarrassed expression that his digimate had contacted him to remind him that he had an appointment at 08:00, which would require fifteen minutes to complete and that he would therefore not be able to meet her until 08:30.

"Was it listening to you, that it knew you were making an appointment with me ?"

Ronin nodded, "We are always connected; it is a requirement for anyone living Upside"

"But, when you came to see me, you—"

Ronin's face stiffened suddenly, and Julia understood he did not want her to say what she had been about to say.

Instead, Ronin said, "When I visited Downside, I wasn't distracted because everyone knew I was occupied with new things that would require my full attention. But my digimate still kept track of me."

Julia's expression indicated she wasn't certain what he had said was the truth, but she did not insist. Instead, she snorted and made a dispirited comment about how much she had to learn about Upside and about whether she'd ever be able to adapt. Ronin took her hand, squeezed it gently, and reminded her that she wouldn't need to adapt to Upside since they'd soon be leaving. She sighed, forced a smile, and the two separated.

After getting to her room, on the hotel's ninety-night floor, unpacking the few things she had, noticing that there were no viewing screens of any kind, and taking a surprisingly soothing shower despite the initial frustration that the operation of the water controls caused her, Julia lay down on a suspensor chair that faced the window and spent several hours thinking about all that she had experienced since arriving Upside—or in the Disk, as they called it.

And her mind whirled, what with worrying about her ability to fit into a society where few used their voices; where she'd be forced to have a brainchip implanted in her to be able to receive her orders or hear people talking who did not wish to use their voices; where she could not tell if someone was a human or a machine; where people could only be together in public, for a business purpose or for a rare personal purpose such as eating a meal together, or—as Ronin had told her while at the restaurant—to attend a concert, which was one of the only events where Upsiders came to truly experience togetherness and sound. Would it be any different on ship? She'd still be surrounded by Ronin's people. But it was not only the people and the culture that made her uneasy. It was also the utter unfamiliarity of the place which glittered outside her windows to reveal shapes and structures she had never even imagined; things she did not recognize or understand. Sure, there were trees and shrubs and flowering plants everywhere; even gurgling ponds. They were beautiful. But it was all artificial. The air, most of all, had a strange quality.

Two things alone comforted her: the fact that she was not as conspicuous anymore—except if one paid attention to her pocked and blemished face—, and the fact that she and Ronin were of a mind about things, though he was an Upsider. This thought reminded her how he had insulted the clerk at the clothing store, and she laughed a good, needed laugh. And having laughed, she was able to finally relax and slump into a welcome slumber.

***

The next morning, at precisely 08:30, Ronin came to get Julia to accompany her to the MPF.

It took twenty minutes for them to reach the location of the escalator to Level 2, the Military level—twenty minutes spent walking, carpeting, and walking and carpeting some more. Julia noticed that the further they got from the Off-worlder section, the more the types, colors and shapes of the individuals surrounding them changed.

Julia followed Ronin to the long escalator, which took visitors and military staff to the Military level. As they engaged on it, the closeness of so many Upsiders sent her heart into a frenetic trot. But she soon understood that people weren't noticing her, now that she wore the local clothes, and she relaxed a little.

From their vantage point, going up the escalator, she realized that she could observe Ronin's strange people without fear, though she was certain that even if she were looking at them straight in the eye, they would barely notice her despite her obvious differences. For indeed, all seemed to be caught up in some otherworldly affair knowable only to them; even Ronin was spending more and more of his time simply staring into nothingness as they approached the facility. So, she studied the multitude—that's what she had decided to call the mixture of people and robots—to try and make sense of them in the tunneled focus of the escalator.

And strange they were. Of course, she had seen Upsiders down on Earth, but never so many and never in all the colors and shades or in the variety as presented themselves to her, now. Perhaps sixty to seventy percent of the individuals she saw must be fully enhanced people—or fullsynths, as Ronin called them—, given the perfection of their bodies, and the unusual skin color of many. In fact, there were people with varied shades of green or brown or blue or white, and those shades were not like the uneven skin tones of her people; these were perfectly uniform and smooth and…and otherworldly. The rest of the multitude she could see ahead must be composed mostly of partially enhanced humans, with normal skin colors, like Ronin. Only a few of them appeared like they must be robots based on the groove she could see at their hairlines. And all were mute and staring into nothingness.

Julia was studying the features of a particularly handsome or beautiful person dressed in military uniform, when the person suddenly turned back to look straight at her. Julia gasped and the moment she did, a dozen of the individuals she had deemed human turned around to look at her. Not a whisper escaped from them to tell her what they thought, but she knew from their looks that they were annoyed at finding a fullhuman amongst them. Ronin, having noticed, moved his hand as slowly as he could to touch hers, to soothe her. When she felt his skin on hers, she held back a whisper of gratitude, then asked herself how long she would have to keep repressing her natural responses.

Surprisingly, everyone who had turned toward her promptly returned to looking into the same nothingness they had been staring at before her disruptive breath. She wondered what they might be thinking or doing now. Were they complaining to someone else or to each other about the noisy fullhuman? Were they working? Sharing information with colleagues? Discussing problems with a supervisor? Or were they planning their day with a spouse? No! they would not be doing that; as Ronin had told her, no one 'coupled' Upside. The statement still frightened her, and she prayed that Ronin was right about this General Genghis, and that they would be able to live together once they got to K'Tara.

When they finally arrived at the top of the long escalator, Ronin sent, *"Over there."* Julia had not heard him, of course, and he almost bumped into her. Ronin excused himself and whispered, "I'm sorry. Sometimes I forget you still don't have your brainchip." He pointed with his chin in the direction of a small spherical building on the side of the larger one she had seen from the spaceport floor on Level 1.

The sight of the structure with its medical symbol dragged a groan from Julia. She had already been subjected to medical procedures twice: once on Earth—just before leaving—to ensure she carried no infectious disease; then upon her arrival Upside, to implant a tracker in her belly; and now, again, to initiate the replacement of her entire bacterial flora—a process that would take several days, but was a requirement for anyone intending to become an Upsider. This had shocked her, not the fact that they would subject people to such a procedure, but that they *had* such a procedure because it meant she was not the only one coming Upside. In fact, she had felt some excitement at the thought. But Ronin had disappointed her when he explained that the procedure was really meant for non-Terran immigrants. The robots—or robodocs—would also perform a complete scan of her body to determine her health condition, and to provide her with a list of organs and other body parts she might wish or need to replace with synthetic or mechanical ones—as if she would have the credits for any of it. One operation that the military *would* pay for was the implantation of a brainchip, but only after she successfully passed her probationary tests. *Probationary tests.* Ronin had tried to explain what those were, and it had not sounded pleasant. Had Ronin felt as lost as she did now when he first went Downside? She wondered.

Entering the medical facility shocked Julia just as much as everything else had, for indeed, in the waiting room, she *heard the sounds of humans*, enhanced or partly enhanced humans coughing or sniffling or simply groaning from the pain they must be feeling. After a moment, though, she felt amusingly relieved that this—the sounds of sick people— made her feel like she was back on Earth. But, that was the limit of the similarity because everyone here seemed to be alone, and only their eyes—staring at the walls—and the infrequent motions of their faces indicated that they were in contact with someone else who was perhaps giving them some emotional support. On Earth, a patient was always accompanied by a family member or friend to comfort them, unless they were homeless.

After Julia took the seat Ronin nodded to, he went to the reception desk. Julia did not hear him speak, but she saw what appeared to be a halfsynth female exchange frustrated motions with two other persons in the office behind her. Finally, passing Ronin, she came to Julia and—with a throaty electronic voice—said, "We do not know what we are supposed to do with you. You will need to wait."

Faces turned their way, staring at her as well as at Ronin. He stared back, and they turned away. As the woman stepped to leave, Julia called to her. The woman stopped and turned, frustration clear on her face.

"I was told you would need to initiate a…bacterial replacement treatment, and scan my body, then—"

"I know why you were sent here. But you have no digital history for us to review and we have no forms for you to fill out. You will need to wait."

So, Julia and Ronin waited, an entire hour.

When the medical clerk finally returned, she said, "I need to download the medical data you accumulated since your arrival, but since you've only been here a day and have no proper digital life yet, you also need to fill out these forms."

Julia took the proffered tablet then touched her finger to another, which the woman held, to download her data. That done, she started answering the lengthy set of questions while the woman returned to her station and called one patient after another to the examination rooms. Her turn did not come too soon; it was now nearly noon, and she had not eaten anything yet.

***

Several times, while waiting by herself in an examination room or with Ronin in the waiting room, Julia asked herself whether she had made a mistake. And when one of the robodocs came and started probing her as if she were just a piece of machinery, she almost cried and wondered whether the robodoc would report her as unfit to be Upside. When she briefly returned to the lobby, she wondered, again, whether she could get used to life among Upsiders despite Ronin's sympathetic, encouraging words. But, while she waited in another examination room, she reminded herself that this was only temporary; that once they reached that far-off planet Ronin kept talking about, they would be able to live a more normal life; a life among fullhumans and on a healthier planet than Earth. That prospect gave her courage and she kept going through the motions, as frustrating as they were.

It was almost mid-afternoon before Julia was done with all the medical procedures. But she *was* finally dismissed from the Medical Center and instructed to get to the Enrollment Facility next door, despite the slight nausea she felt from the bacterial replacement procedure. As they stood to leave, Julia re-read the robodoc's report and shook her head. The document said that she should replace her eyes and her pancreas! She wanted to ask Ronin what crazy thing that was. But she knew she could not make a scene, so she turned off the tablet and stuffed it in her back pocket with another shaking of her head while Ronin told her she would need to keep the tablet and take it everywhere she went from now on, unless she got an arm replaced with a mechanical one which would have a digidisplay in it. She almost barked a "What the f***!" at that suggestion. For the first time since they arrived Upside, Ronin laughed—a real, loud laugh—and Julia almost shouted with indignation when she saw the grin on his face. Of course, the nurses and patients glared at them, and they left while Ronin excused himself. The two of them continued to laugh together as they walked. It had felt good, so very good to let go of the stress, even if just for a minute.

Some ten meters away from the Enrollment Facility, however, Julia stopped and turned to Ronin with an expression of tense apprehension. She said, "This is it." Then, she studied Ronin's face, to see whether he still believed her coming Upside and joining the General's mission with him was a good idea. She could tell from his expression that he was torn about it, perhaps because of all the stress she had experienced since coming up here.

When he replied, it was with some tension in his voice and a tentative, hopeful smile on his face, "Yes, this is it. Are you ready?"

Julia took a deep, shuddering breath, swallowed, then nodded yes. They went in.

***

Julia's processing by the army of military staff and officers who sent her first here and then there just to be sent back here and there again nearly caused her a nervous breakdown. And she did not need to tell Ronin when she rejoined him in the waiting room; he could tell.

61

Whispering, Ronin told her how he had felt when he joined, over a year ago; it had been frustrating and humiliating. In fact, he had asked himself more than once whether the army was staffed with idiots. And sometime during his second month as a trainee, a realization hit him out of left field: the induction process, the seemingly idiotic officers and civilian staff, it was all *meant* to be that way; to weed out right from the start those who could not deal with chaos—the chaos which those who stayed would surely meet in war. Julia wasn't so sure about Ronin's reasoning, but she supposed she would find out for herself.

After being questioned by three sergeants, being sent to five different rooms to be subjected to tests she did not even know existed, and filling out eight different questionnaires, Julia finally returned to Ronin with a flustered, discombobulated expression.

"They didn't tell me anything except to remain in the complex and to report to the Incoming Facility tomorrow at 07:00. And they have a room for me at the Imperial Praetorian."

When a smile appeared on Ronin's face where she had expected sympathy, she asked him why and—for the first time since he brought her Upside—he spoke with an excited voice, "Do you know what this means?"

Numb as she was, she still guessed at the answer and hope bloomed on her own face.

***

Two weeks after Julia's arrival on the Disk, she and Ronin were waiting with the growing lines of military and civilian crewmembers to embark on the Galactic, on this 13th day of January 4631 AD. And although they had been waiting for two hours already, the breathtaking nature of the vessel they were waiting to board mesmerized her. But what fascinated her even more was the nervous anticipation she felt in everyone around her, Ronin included.

Wondering what had everyone so anxious, she whispered a question to Ronin.

He replied in the same manner, "General Genghis and Empress Alia will be giving a speech in thirty minutes."

Julia gave a little snort and Ronin's bunkmate, who was standing to Ronin's right and whom she had finally met as they gathered here, said a little bluntly, "You've never heard them? Not even via diginection?"

Julia resisted a desire to challenge Dovard's tone and shook her head to say 'no'.

Dovard cocked his eyes, and it seemed to Julia that he knew something about her *she* didn't know. She looked to Ronin who made a dismissive motion toward his friend, and she returned to observing the growing spectacle.

A few rows ahead of them, a person turned around and locked gazes with Julia. Her heart froze. She recognized the individual; it was the one who looked at her when she was going up the escalator, the day of her arrival. Julia struggled to tear her eyes away. What did it—ey—want? Why did ey keep looking at her? She exhaled a long, relieved breath when the person finally let go of her.

It was now precisely 12:30, and a chirp sounded in the brainchip of every single person in attendance for the departure of the Galactic. As one single creature, Ronin and everyone else turned their heads toward the stage—except for Julia who hadn't heard anything.

Julia wondered what was happening and wanted to ask Ronin. However, seeing how entranced everyone was with she knew-not-what, she decided to keep her question for later and to do as they were doing. But it was so frustrating to not be able to hear what the others heard. Were they hearing music? A speech? No one was yet on stage except for an individual putting the final touches to…to microphones. *So, there* is *going to be loud speaking?*

All Julia's complaints vanished when she heard almost everyone around her gasp. She looked at Ronin with a question on her face, when she saw two supernatural people walk on stage. Were they the General and the Empress? *Of course. Who else? You've seen their photos.* Arguing with herself, she thought: *But they look like gods.* The other part of herself replied: *Yes, the gods who tolerate the continued wasting of our people.* Julia shook that upsetting thought and returned to watching the unfolding spectacle.

A powerful, otherworldly voice now blared across the spaceport, "Defenders of Alia's Empire!"

Genghis's first words, spoken aloud, and the accompanying martial music drew moans from every single person in the audience. But after a brief moment, Ronin shook his head in anger.

Julia turned to him.

He whispered, "Events like this," he spread his arms to show the people and then pointed to his ears, "are really rare. So rare that," Ronin paused while working the words out, "the mere anticipation sends shivers in our bones, and then—the hearing—it shakes us." Ronin took a frustrated breath and added, "I shouldn't be reacting this way; none of us should. I wish I could just turn off my senses and my brain right now, but I can't."

Having heard his comrade, Dovard lifted a knowing brow and said, "It's just biology, Ronin; biology and technology."

Ronin sighed gloomily.

Dovard looked at Ronin as if he must be speaking to him, but no words came out. Noticing Julia's question, he switched to audible speech, "I am sorry, Julia. I was telling Ronin he…should be happy he can at least turn off outgoing communications when he wants to."

Julia bobbed her head, and Ronin swallowed whatever other remark he had been about to make.

On stage, General Genghis, Proconsul of Earth and of its Colonies, stood with a radiant smile, cheering everyone with his arms raised toward the darkness above; he was certainly aware of the effect of his speech and of the music. After letting the fifty thousand soldiers and civilians feel the pleasure of the sounds until they demanded more with their rapt gazes and moans, he continued, "You are here assembled and ready to board the Galactic, because there is a revolt," he waved behind himself as a projection appeared on the ship's surface, "a revolt wreaking havoc on Kepler, a revolt which will grow beyond the planet, and which it is our duty to quell so that the rest of Kepler's inhabitants, and the rest of us, may continue to know the Empress's goodwill."

A voice seemingly out of nowhere now asked, loudly, demandingly, "But why must we intervene?"

And a perfectly modulated voice—the most perfect in all the galaxy—answered the question with an ecstatic effect on the audience, "Because we are a connected race, and poison in one organ harms the entire body."

Empress Alia paused for effect then intoned, "Citizens of Earth, you are my arms, my legs, my heart! Therefore, go and set!"

The audience broke into a chant lifted by music until it reached even First and Third Levels of the Disk. The audience—whether humans, fullsynths, halfsynths, or synthetics—responded as one, as they had all learned or been programmed to respond, despite any objection any of them may have had to the Empress's Grand Plan. They chanted, "Because we are citizens of Earth, we will go and set! Because we are citizens of Earth, we will go and set! Because we are…"

Julia turned to Ronin, terrorized and afraid that he too might be caught in the mad chant.

But something pulled him back from the abyss of the unwelcome rapture, and—after shooting a worried glance at Dovard—he turned to Julia, his voice shaky and angry. "I really can't wait to be done with this place."

To be Continued

THE AUTHOR

L.A. Di Paolo is a tri-lingual, Canadian-born Italian American who lives in Milton, Vermont. By day, because of his background in science and business, he manages drug development projects. By night, he writes and the constant questions trotting in his mind are those about evolution, nature, and the human condition. He has been writing to explore them and their answers, first in student newspapers, then in a magazine he authored and published, and now in his novel.

If you are interested in learning more about L.A. Di Paolo or about this novel, you can visit his author web site at https://ladipaolo.net, or scan the QR Code below.

9 7989899 2038811